TOO MUCH BLOODY NOISE

TOO MUCH BLOODY NOISE

Eleanor Berry

The Book Guild Ltd

First published in Great Britain in 2023 by
The Book Guild Ltd
Unit E2 Airfield Business Park,
Harrison Road, Market Harborough,
Leicestershire. LE16 7UL
Tel: 0116 2792299
www.bookguild.co.uk
Email: info@bookguild.co.uk
Twitter: @bookguild

Copyright © 2023 Eleanor Berry

The right of Eleanor Berry to be identified as the author of this
work has been asserted by them in accordance with the
Copyright, Design and Patents Act 1988.

All rights reserved. No part of this publication may be
reproduced, transmitted, or stored in a retrieval system, in any form or by any means,
without permission in writing from the publisher, nor be otherwise circulated in
any form of binding or cover other than that in which it is published and without
a similar condition being imposed on the subsequent purchaser.

This work is entirely fictitious and bears no resemblance to any persons living or dead.

Typeset in 11pt Baskerville

Printed and bound in Great Britain by 4edge Limited

ISBN 978 1915853 509

British Library Cataloguing in Publication Data.
A catalogue record for this book is available from the British Library.

For my sister, Harriet.

Too Much Bloody Noise

"Who's ringing that blasted bell?" The front door of the large semi-detached house in Knightsbridge was being rung persistently. The inhabitants of the house were known as the Stratisfords.

Hilary, the eldest daughter, and her husband were middle-aged. Her husband, a Frenchman called Jean-Pierre Dupont, was wealthy and hailed from the Rive Droite in Paris. Hilary and Jean-Pierre were having lunch and were talking animatedly about painters. History of art was their favourite subject, and they spoke about it almost all the time during meals, even during breakfast.

Apart from art, the couple talked about Roman poetry, French poetry, and the works of other classical writers. Overall, they were regarded as being bluestockings.

Mauro, their Portuguese butler, invariably wore a starched white jacket, when he passed food round the table. He opened the dining-room door and carried the second course, on which fruit salad had been prepared.

"Hilary's younger sister, Natalie, has just arrived in a

red Porsche. She wishes to speak to you on a matter of some weight," said Mauro.

"What about?" asked Hilary impatiently.

Suddenly, a woman wearing a red leather suit stormed towards Hilary. She had blonde layered hair, unlike Hilary's black hair.

Hilary's husband, Jean-Pierre Dupont, was extremely wealthy.

"What do you want?" asked Hilary aggressively.

Natalie looked nonplussed.

"I want to know where my Michael's ashes have been put. I want to know now!"

"Let's go into the garden first," said Hilary angrily.

The two sisters walked into the garden and sat down under an oak tree.

"I'm afraid I don't know where they've been put," Hilary commented mildly, and giggled nervously. She had had quite a lot of wine before lunch. She hiccupped and called vaguely for Mauro, who rushed towards her, like the rabbit in *Alice in Wonderland*.

"I demand to know where my brother's ashes are," Natalie said repeatedly.

"I'm not entirely sure where they were laid, after his funeral. It's just possible someone may have put them under the willow tree near the river," muttered Mauro, after looking at his mistress.

"Who would have put them under a bloody willow tree?" shouted Natalie.

"Must you use such tactless language?" bellowed Hilary. "This is England, and in England, we often cremate our bloody dead. We don't put them into the earth."

The two sisters made more noise in their garden than in their house.

Despite their proximity, the neighbours heard every word uttered. Hence the family were referred to as "some of the most noisy people alive".

The Stratisfords allowed even Natalie to stay with them for a while. Michael was her favourite brother. Even his ashes were found eventually, in an extraordinarily unlikely place, namely the bottom of a potting shed.

The sisters found the whereabouts of the ashes a disagreeable topic, and as they had recently suffered from horrible bereavements, they spoke about other subjects.

The neighbours owned a large, red-brick vicarage, covered in places by stained-glass windows. Arthur Hetherington, the vicar, a burly chap, his wife, Priscilla, his four children, two boys and two girls, and his array of black Labrador dogs, all occupied the premises. The family also owned unused croquet lawns, a tennis court, and a swimming pool.

It was a stifling Sunday afternoon when the Hetherington family were particularly upset. They had been playing tennis, during which the children had been asked to act as ball boys.

Those who did not wish to join in, because of the heat, went to the swimming pool.

The outer gate of the tennis court was adjacent to the Stratisfords' thick front door. The Reverend could take no more. He threw his weight violently against the door and knocked it off its hinges, as if he had been a member of the *Gestapo*.

The furious Frenchman's first reaction was to punch the burly Reverend on the jaw, knowing that the Man of the Cloth would soon have to replace the broken-down door.

Hilary used characteristically loud language and, as was always customary in her case, her voice carried all over the house. She broke into Latin at one point, and ostentatiously recited thirty lines of Virgil, while Natalie had nervous hysterical giggles.

It was not until the Reverend had actually kicked the Stratisfords' door to the floor that he noticed the door's colour, and the street number as well.

The family lived at 112 Crescent Road, and their front door was a bright shade of blue.

The Reverend only made a note of the door's colour after he had fallen face downwards onto the Persian carpets covering the hall. He had also knocked out two of his false teeth.

"You're completely mad!" said Hilary, adding, "I am prepared to pay for you to receive psychiatric therapy, if only to let us all have some peace!"

The Reverend struggled to get to his feet. "You're a fine one to talk about peace!" he muttered. "Sometimes, you all make enough noise to wake the dead.

"I am prepared to receive therapy from your family's purse, to make this neighbourhood quieter all round," the Reverend said pompously, when it was the Stratisfords who had made the bulk of the noise in the first place.

Hetherington continued, "I am also going to repair the two teeth which you so clumsily knocked out. Kindly give me your dentist's name and address."

"My dentist has rooms at 120 Harley Street," said Hilary spontaneously.

"What's his name?" asked the Reverend curtly.

"It is Mr Harvey, and his rooms are on the second floor. His phone number is 0207-935-8502. I will explain to him that you had an accident and lost two front teeth."

Hilary was afraid of attracting more attention than she had already. She went out into the street and hailed a taxi which turned up within about ten minutes and another, whose driver she told to go to her personal therapist. She sought his services at least four times a week. His name was Mr Douglas Cumberbatch.

After all the sisters did not wish to make enemies with a *Man of the Cloth*, even if he were Anglican, as opposed to Catholic. Nor indeed did Jean-Pierre, who had made just as much noise as she had at meals, when the couple had been arguing so feverishly.

The Reverend was just as tactless as they were, and he had a lot of trouble with his staff, particularly with his butler and cook. Many members of his staff handed in their notice, due to inadequate payment, over a long period of time.

It did not help matters, when one of the Reverend's daughters (Alice, aged ten) crept up behind the butler in the pantry and put her hand on his bottom, for comic relief. Neither the butler nor the Reverend found the gesture funny.

The Reverend remained permanently at war with his foul-tempered butler and cook.

Some of the children sang a humorous song called *The Farmer and the Cowman Should Be Friends* from the musical

Oklahoma. Neither the Reverend nor his frail wife, Priscilla, found any part of the song even remotely amusing.

The Reverend continued to say an extensive grace before meals, however. Also, his wife and children refused to participate.

It was the Reverend himself who did the carving at lunch and dinner, and the overworked Priscilla, who cooked and did the washing up after meals.

The Reverend's Sunday sermons dwindled as did his congregations. Finally, he was disciplined by not just one but two Bishops. He turned to large quantities of alcohol and consumed at least two bottles of whisky per day.

It was not long before he was defrocked. His temper worsened, and he and Priscilla divorced within twenty months.

The Reverend's four children had grown well into their late teens and had unsuccessfully sought employment. Unlike their father, they loafed and basically did nothing, other than turn to drugs, many of which were hard.

They took up shoplifting. The eldest member of the family, a young man called Cedric, burgled stately homes, allowed himself to be caught and served lengthy custodial sentences.

Hence, the Reverend was left on his own. All his children had deserted him, and Priscilla had nothing to do with him. In the end, she was admitted to a sordid old people's home, stenched with urine.

The Reverend could tolerate his solitude no more. One autumn morning, he tiptoed to the Stratisfords' house, where Hilary, Natalie and Jean-Pierre were having breakfast.

"What are you doing here?" they all said simultaneously.

The Reverend ruffled his thick brown hair, as well as his dusty dog collar.

"I'll come straight to the point, without preamble," said the Reverend. "My wife has divorced me and is in an old people's home. My four children have gone on to hard drugs and are in prison. I am totally alone."

As Jean-Pierre had once been a well-known therapist, it was not unnatural for him to take pity on an impoverished, homeless party.

Also, Natalie was a brilliant raconteur, as well as an academic, even more than her sister. "You've come to the right place," she commented sympathetically. "She and I have a lot of amusing stories."

"I like amusing stories," said the Reverend.

Natalie felt slightly left out of Hilary's stories. She crept out of the drawing room and up the back stairs, while Hilary told a few more raucous stories.

Natalie went to the nursery and opened a box containing some letters in which an American had accounted for his no longer wishing to see her.

A cleaner, who had once been a nanny, was trying to tidy up after Natalie and Hilary. There were some more boxes containing letters and the stars and stripes, which Natalie had once strewn on the floor, in a fit of rage. This was when Natalie's relationship with her former American lover had been going strong, before it had disintegrated.

"Do you want to keep these flags, Miss Natalie?" asked the cleaner, while picking up some of the flags.

"No! Get those filthy sanitary towels out of my sight!"

shouted the fiery young girl. She threw them into the unfortunate cleaner's face and ran downstairs.

In the meantime, the Reverend pottered around the gardens. All he could see was a long, dirty table, covered with cobwebs and dust.

It was also possible to see the odd candlestick, cobweb-caked with dribbling wax.

He was happy for the first time in years, because he no longer had a family to call his own. All his family had walked out on him.

Also, Natalie allowed him to plaster the walls of the spare room with dark red and gold, which gave it an ecclesiastical tone. It gave him so much pleasure to look at the ceiling and walls as well.

Whenever the Reverend lay on his back, he could see these things and be happier still. He was not charged any rent either.

However, the Stratisfords made just as much noise as they had over the years, and gave birth to two noisy but charming sons. They were twins, called William and Harold, and they were always fighting. The Reverend had become even more contented and enjoyed making as much noise as his hosts.

The Reverend was equally as academic as his hosts and continued to be well versed in Latin and Greek. He said lengthy graces in Latin, whether his hosts cared for them to be said or not.

On one Saturday morning, the twins, aged about fourteen, had a violent fight, using the rungs of the bannisters. Their bone of contention appeared to be a woman. They pulled the rungs out of their sockets. Natalie was walking by and saw William lying on his back, holding one of the sockets in his mouth, with Harold on top of him.

The twins ended up lying on the floor for a while, while blood oozed from their mouths. A passing maid, who looked at the scene, fainted. Hilary made them pay for the broken rungs out of their pocket money.

The next time the family, including the delighted Reverend, had gathered together was Christmas Day. Both the Reverend and Natalie shared some of Jean-Pierre's recreational drugs, and Jean-Pierre told one naughty story after another. The only people who did not partake were Hilary and the twins.

William had left his supply of insulin (for diabetes) in the flat which he shared with Harold, in London.

Before Christmas lunch, he paced up and down, like an expectant father, and made extensive calls to various doctors, regardless of the fact that most of them would be away from their offices on Christmas Day.

Natalie was very upset by William's pacing. She adored the twins and couldn't bear it when one of them was distressed.

"What is it, my boy? Why are you pacing up and down like that?" she asked.

"Oh, I'm just very excited because it's Christmas," said her nephew.

Natalie had an alternative sense of humour, and laughed out loud but, at the same time, wept within. During lunch, William picked up his mobile and made yet another call. He did this throughout lunch.

"When you make these calls, you really must give your name first," Natalie called out kindly.

It took the wretched boy over an hour to get through to A&E in a neighbouring town. Also, it took him forty-five minutes to get hold of a taxi.

Once he had taken his insulin, he was able to get through a portion of turkey, followed by Christmas pudding, and was able to speak once more.

"The trouble with you is, you always live on a knife's edge, Bro," commented Harold mildly.

"You're absolutely right, Bro," agreed William.

"I can't bear seeing you suffering so much, my boy," said Natalie. "It would be better if you were to bring all your stuff to the house at the same time."

***

During Christmas Day, Natalie took amphetamines in small doses, and spoke at length about Russian literature, starting with a comparison between Tolstoy and Dostoevsky.

She knew a lot about this subject (as did Hilary), mainly because of its moribund tones.

"Not very long ago, when I was in Moscow," began Natalie, "I overheard a conversation between two young women on the metro, comparing Tolstoy and Dostoevsky. Let me refer to them as Olga and Masha"

'I'll talk about Tolstoy, now,' said Masha, assertively.

'Oh, the refreshingly westernised Tolstoy!' she added.

'I can liken him to a mountain stream in Midsummer,' she continued passionately.

Natalie took a deep breath and suddenly broke into a strange cockney accent.

"Oh, I tell a lie!" she suddenly stated for effect, adding, "I left out the long passage about this fucking dickhead called Pierre Bazukov! (From *War and Peace.*) This idiot runs in front of the cannons of *Borodino*, brandishing binoculars, wearing civvies and shouting about his bloody immortal soul! Many advanced Russian students liken Pierre Bazukov to Tolstoy himself," Natalie added as an afterthought.

"Olga argued that she preferred Dostoevsky to Tolstoy, because Dostoevsky's works were more intense in places, and were occasionally preoccupied with sickness and unhappiness.

"The same woman was referring to certain passages in *Crime and Punishment*, when its hero, Raskolnikov, was frequently ill and lived in a garret.

"Raskolnikov went to bed in his clothes one night, and his cleaner commented, 'Why, you've been to bed in your clothes, sir. What a *sad* man you must be!'

"Olga was able to put some work into *The Idiot* and *The Brothers Karamazov*, to which she gave equal coverage."

Natalie was stuffed with more amphetamines and ignored desperate pleas from her sister to stop dominating the conversation.

She ignored her sister and banged the table. There was a pause, broken by Hilary.

"For Christ's sake, shut up, Natalie! You simply can't dominate the conversation by carrying on about bloody Russian literature all the way through lunch!"

Jean-Pierre, who had also taken amphetamines, but to a lesser extent than Natalie, spoke at length about Greek mythology. The subject bored Natalie. Hilary, however, asked him erudite questions about ancient Greece.

After lunch and coffee was served, Hilary, who was very angry with Natalie, got up and left the table, followed by the Reverend and his dogs. Natalie walked forward and stroked one of them. She followed her sister into the drawing room.

"I'd like a word with you," said Hilary.

"About what?"

"Have you been taking bloody amphetamines again? Dr Festenstein, our doctor, said how dangerous it is to take them in large doses."

"Mind your own business! Besides, Jean-Pierre takes them. He said so."

"What Jean-Pierre takes and what you take have nothing at all to do with the matter!"

The younger sister did not know that the older sister had any idea at all about the hidden whereabouts of her precious stash of amphetamines. She stormed out of the drawing room and went to her bedroom. She was shattered. She went through one drawer after another and underneath the mattress, through every part of her cupboards, and even tried to take up the floorboards with a screwdriver.

Natalie's supply could not be found anywhere. Even her attempts to locate some of the drugs among Jean-Pierre's possessions bitterly failed.

She was gutted and approached her sister.

"I want my drugs back, Hilary. They are my property."

"I can't give them to you, unless you ask Dr Festenstein to do so. Only he and he alone will give them to you. You have been taking them for far too long."

"I will make an appointment to see him then. I need the drugs to help me write my books."

"He may not agree, Natalie."

Dr Festenstein was unwell for the next week or two. Natalie was admitted to a smart clinic in North London. No one knew exactly where Dr Festenstein was at the time.

Once Natalie was admitted to a clinic in north London, she did not have any withdrawal symptoms at first. Neither she nor Hilary knew how terrible Natalie's symptoms would be, particularly when the drug was taken in large quantities.

Also, Hilary did not know how many amphetamines her sister had been taking, and that, if they had been withdrawn suddenly, withdrawal could lead to incomparable depression of an almost catatonic nature.

Apart from that, the patient in question can suffer from major epileptic fits and could easily swallow their tongue. Fortunately, Natalie was able to speak to Dr Festenstein, eventually. Festenstein rang up the clinic but was still unwell.

He referred Natalie to a sadistically inclined psychiatric consultant, who did not believe in prescribing any medication at all, even for urinary tract infections. His name was Dr Hanning, and he took eight holidays a year, mainly in the Bahamas!

Hilary, Jean-Pierre, and the Reverend visited Natalie every day, and stared hopelessly at her motionless eyes. On her tenth day under Dr Hanning's care, Natalie was more than suicidally depressed. She waited for her guests to leave, climbed off the roof of the clinic, into the shrubbery, despite her terrible fear of heights, and threw herself to the ground.

When Dr Hanning found out, all he could say to his patient was that the episode was "damned embarrassing". He also traumatised her sister at two o'clock in the morning and told her that Natalie had given his department a thoroughly "bad name".

Natalie still craved the amphetamines from which she had been withdrawing. Hanning did nothing to alleviate Natalie's situation, and she swallowed her tongue yet again.

She was taken to another hospital. When she had finally withdrawn from amphetamines, she discharged herself, put on decent clothes, and eventually sued Dr Hanning, whose sadism caused him to be struck off.

Natalie returned to Dr Festenstein, befriended him once more and complained bitterly about her ordeal at the clinic. He assured her that the taking of amphetamines was justified but in moderation only.

Hilary, too, consulted Dr Festenstein, and he told her that she had almost ended her sister's life.

To compensate, Natalie refrained from talking about Russian literature during meals, and the two dogmatic sisters were reconciled.

In the meantime, Natalie hid her stash of amphetamines in a large safe in her bedroom, just in case Hilary chose to raid it. However, Hilary promised not to do so.

Dr Festenstein referred Natalie to a much more civilised Harley Street psychiatrist, who did not find a lot wrong with her. The only factor amiss with his new patient was her morbid obsession with whether or not he suffered from ill health. His name was Dr Zelder.

He wrote a long and extremely amusing letter to Dr Festenstein, stating, "At first, I was unable to assess Natalie's state of mind. All she did during her hour's consultation was cross-examine me about the state of my health, and in particular my liver.

"This leads me to suspect that she could possibly have suffered from a number of bereavements at some time or another.

"However, Natalie explained that she had been taking amphetamines in small doses and had lived in naked fear of having her supply taken away from her by her sister with the best will in the world. She needs access to the drug because she is a writer and could not manage to write without them."

Dr Zelder continued, at enormous length, that Natalie Klein had obsessive-compulsive disorder but is not without a sense of humour. During her second consultation with Dr Zelder, she accounted for an incident during the German invasion of Russia during World War Two.

She told the psychiatrist about a certain Herr Hochenhauser, a monocled General, who was intensely depressed by the monotonous and endless steppe lands which rolled before him. The General was unable to take any more of the horribly bleak steppe lands, and in the end, he felt suicidal.

He made one hysterical call after another to Berlin, and ordered ten crates filled with amphetamines, on the grounds that the drug was readily available throughout Germany.

Due to his rank, and his loud, carrying voice, he was amply supplied with ten crates, but not once did he share any of his copious booty with his desperate comrades.

Natalie laughed out loud. "I survive by black humour," she confessed.

"I'll tell you another joke," said she, just before the end of that particular consultation. "I have terrible trouble understanding films, because I am slightly deaf. I always ask other people around me what is going on.

"Apparently, Stalin's senior minister, Molotov, had the same problem. He asked Stalin one question after another during films, and he must have driven the old man insane. However, probably from the sheer goodness of his heart, Stalin failed to reply to any of Molotov's questions."

Natalie laughed and laughed and went on laughing. "It was really decent of Stalin not to have pulled the trigger," she added.

"Hey! Hey! Hey! I've just cracked a bloody hilarious joke! You're supposed to laugh, goddamnit!" said Natalie.

"Had you been taking amphetamines during all our previous consultations?" asked Dr Zelder.

"Well, sometimes," replied the patient.

"In that case, I hope you will tell me more anecdotes next time we meet, but I must insist that you do so in moderation, repeat, moderation."

***

"I've got another story for you," said Natalie. "Also, the drugs were in moderation.

"My mother, Lady Kitty Stratisford, was just as eccentric as I am," she began.

"Was she quite as eccentric as you are?" asked Dr Zelder.

"Yes."

"Did she also take a lot of pills?"

"No, I don't think she did. She was very conservative though"

"When she was young, she went to Russia, under Stalin's rule, and was even more dotty than I am.

"She accompanied my father on the trans-Siberian railway.

"As the train passed through the steppe lands, she shouted at the top of her voice: 'God, this is an ugly country! Oh, this is such an ugly country!' An English-speaking guide was sitting next to her!

"Incidentally, I was reminded of the story about the gloomy German general."

She continued, as before. "Can you *beat the phenomenal* ugliness of this country?

"This was not the end. She got off at Vladivostok where she had a man shot!

"This wasn't her worst. Before she got off the train, she saw some ragged children in the street, and said, very loudly, 'Why are these children running about in rags? I thought this was meant to be a socialist country?!'"

Natalie and Dr Zelder laughed once more. Natalie added, "My father had a lot of stories about the evil Beria. (He was the Head of Stalin's Secret Police.) I always called him 'Bright Button Beriwinkle'. His main hobby was picking up 12-year-old girls in his limousine at night. He took them to his flat, where he played The First Movement of Rachmaninov's 1st movement of his second Piano Concerto in C minor on the turntable. To put the girls at their ease, he told them that he often wept on hearing the piece, when he was alone.

"He raped one of the girls and terrified her. She screamed her head off. In his *memoirs* the delightful old rogue stated that he was actually 'obliged' to put a cushion over her face to stifle her screams. It had to be 'obliged – not anything else, just obliged'"

"Do you always use this drug when you consult me," repeated Dr Zelder.

"Yes. I've told you this before."

"That is because I am of a melancholy disposition, and I would like to laugh straight away, if I can."

"I don't see why that can't be arranged.

"When did you start taking it Dr Zelder?"

"I would say I started to take it at least twenty years ago," said the psychiatrist, "but in moderation only, like yourself."

***

The people living next door but one occupied a large hospital, which increased in size every year. The more it increased, the greater the number of departments were.
Just out of interest, when the Reverend was walking past the hospital on his usual afternoon walk, he noticed a festival referred to as "View Day". The festival was known as Smithfield Hospital View Day, and usually it took place much earlier in the summer, but for some unknown reason, it took place later this year.

The Reverend was intrigued by a myriad of stalls, which sold T-shirts, bearing the hospital's name on them, books describing the history of the hospital, and black stalls, as well as postcards which were framed in black and white.

Other stalls sold cakes, buns, and chocolates. The Reverend saw men in striped trousers and long black coats, which he had never seen before. He did not know that these men were consultants, at the top of the medical ladder.

He turned round and looked at the dark stone architecture behind him. He saw a much younger man, aged about forty, obviously keen on the music of the late 50s and early 60s, who had just walked through the hospital's main gates, towards the festival.

The man was smiling inanely and making exaggerated rock 'n' roll movements. His name and rank were printed on his lapel. He was known as Julius Rookwood, Senior Hospital Administrator. Everybody knew him as the "Rocker", because he was unable to control his extraordinary movements, particularly when he was nervous.

The "Rocker" rocked all the way to where the cake-eating consultants were standing. The Reverend stood nearby, intrigued by what the Rocker was about to say, if anything.

When the "Rocker" spoke, he showed a heavy Yorkshire accent and, curiously, never used the definite article.

"Gentlemen, are you able to attend a board meeting tomorrow morning?"

"What's all this in aid of, Julius? I do wish you'd stand still," said one of the consultants. "You've hardly given us enough time, have you?"

"11 o'clock sharp," said the "Rocker", breaking nervously into rock 'n' roll movements once more.

The consultants muttered among themselves. They agreed that 11 o'clock would be a reasonably convenient time, after all.

"What do you really want, Julius?" said another consultant.

The "Rocker" raised his voice because his nervousness had increased yet again, and his movements had become even more pronounced, as had his heavy Yorkshire accent. He spoke once more, his voice even more raised than before.

"There's an awful lot of necrophilia going on in mortuary!" he shouted. "I know it's bloomin' rude, but it's a soobject that's got to be addressed."

"Where is the mortuary?" asked the Reverend, out of curiosity.

"Just turn round, facing gate. Before you get to gate, turn left, go down steps and ring bell," said the "Rocker".

The Reverend failed to answer. He left the hospital and strolled along the road and went to the Stratisfords' house, where he stayed for a few days. It was after about three months that he became rather bored with his hosts. He wondered whether he should seek a lady's hand, although his feelings were only chancing.

He found walking in the streets a pleasurable pastime, particularly during the autumn. He liked to walk past secretaries' offices for some of the time and look at the girls through the glass windows. In particular, he liked to look at their legs.

Sometimes, the girls came out of the alleys and onto the pavements, to smoke. There was one girl who came out more frequently than the others. She was unusually tall with long, red hair, and she came out onto the pavement at least once a minute! The Reverend was unable to take his eyes off her. She always wore a red miniskirt and a silk white blouse.

Although her clothing was unchanged from one day to the next, the Reverend felt unbelievably shy whenever he looked at her. Eventually, he plucked up the courage to speak to her one morning and was overjoyed by the fact that he was no longer wearing a dusty dog collar.

"Hullo," he ventured, in a very shy tone of voice.

"Well, hello there."

"Would you care to cross the road and have a drink in the local? It's quite close to where I live."

The Reverend suddenly realised that he had expressed himself clumsily.

"Oh, dear, I wasn't very polite just then. I'm so sorry."

"That's all right."

"What's your name, by the way?"

"Marion McManus."

They sat down and had a gin and tonic each, but Marion only had one, accompanied by a cigarette.

"What do you do in the evenings? Do you have a boyfriend?" asked the Reverend.

"Sometimes I go out with boys," said Marion. "But on the whole, I like to have dinner with my father."

It wasn't long before Marion introduced the Reverend to her father. However, it took her a considerable time to tell her suitor that her father was an undertaker.

Marion was in bed one Friday morning, accompanied by the sleeping Reverend. The phone rang at seven-thirty.

"Who the hell is it?" asked Marion angrily.

"It's your father, actually," said a voice.

"This is a bit steep, isn't it?" said Marion. "I don't have to arrive at the office until nine o'clock."

"All right, all right. I haven't seen you for three weeks now. It's time I saw you for dinner. How about tonight?"

"I'm seeing Vicky tonight."

"What about my seeing you tomorrow night, then? I hear you've got a boyfriend with you. Why can't you bring him tomorrow night?"

"Well, after that, I'm going to an office party."

"Cancel your bloody office party, Marion!" shouted Marion's father, adding, "Even if you are over twenty-one, I still have the power to confiscate your flat! I'm expecting you and your fancy fellow tomorrow night."

"I must say, you are an awful bully, Daddy, but just to please you, I'll bring him with me."

"Good girl. That's what I like to hear."

"My father's an undertaker," said Marion crisply. The Reverend wore a suitable dog collar. Unbeknown to the Reverend, the offices and residential quarters of Marion's father were overbearing, ostentatious and indescribably vulgar.

Marion's father was known as Mr McManus. They had been designated by an American architect hired by Mr McManus himself.

The offices were on the ground floor, and the front room was peppered with giant-sized Madonnas and Childs, their heads encircled by crude, glittering, gold halos, with glass tears on their cheeks, which were turned on all day and all night.

The Reverend, though a lapsed Protestant, found the general appearance of the Catholic ambiance both threatening and frightening, and it greatly increased his dread of meeting Marion's father.

"My father, Mr McManus, will be on the second floor," said Marion stiffly. They both got into a lift, which moved with a pronounced jolt.

The door opened automatically on the second floor. A white-coated, bow-tied servant ushered them into an almost surreal room, its walls covered with mirrors and its upright chairs made of glittering glass once more.

"Welcome back, Miss Marion," said the servant. "Nice to see you after so long."

Marion took off her suede coat (a gift from her father).

"Thank you," she said.

The servant turned to the clergyman. "Welcome to the premises, sir," he said.

"I have it in mind that you're a little daunted by the prospect of meeting Mr McManus," said the servant. "Allow me to let you know that his bark's very much worse than his bite."

"Just how bad is his bark?" ventured the Reverend.

Mr McManus strolled into the room and faced the couple. He was tall and well-built, and aged about sixty. His features were handsome, and his hair was streaked with grey. His voice was quite carrying, and he spoke with a harsh Northern Irish accent.

He was holding half a glass of whisky in his right hand and was wearing a white, linen suit, a pale blue shirt and an arresting red and black tie.

"Ah, Marion," he said, fixing his daughter with a penetrating stare.

"Hullo, Daddy. This is the Reverend, although he refuses to give his name. He is a Protestant."

"I am most honoured to meet you, sir," said the Reverend.

Mr McManus beckoned to his servant.

"Give this man a drink," he commanded.

The servant did so. The whisky relaxed the Reverend's nerves. The host sat on another glass chair. Despite the proximity between host and guest Mr McManus shouted at him throughout the conversation.

"There are two things wrong with you, sir. First, you're British. Second, you're drunk."

"I'm drunk because I'm very nervous, sir, but being British is no fault of mine."

"Why are you a Protestant?"

"I suppose that's the way I was brought up, sir."

"I take it you're familiar with my business. Do you know anything about funerals?"

"Funerals?"

"Yes, funerals. You must know what funerals are. They're those ceremonies which take place after we die."

The Reverend flushed.

"Come on, sir. That means you don't know anything at all about funeral direction?"

"I don't really understand, sir." By now, the empty glass was shaking in the Reverend's hand. Mr McManus appeared exasperated.

"Have you ever been to a funeral, young man?"

"Yes. My father's."

"When did he die?"

"When I was quite young, sir."

Mr McManus poured himself another drink and put the empty bottle on the table once more.

"Burial or cremation?" he shouted.

"I beg your pardon, sir?"

"You really are a slow man. Was he buried or was he cremated?"

"He was buried, sir."

"Sandalwood or pine?" bellowed the undertaker.

The Reverend felt nauseated.

"I'm very sorry, but I don't really understand your question, sir," he muttered.

"Oh, you're so deaf and slow! Was the coffin made of sandalwood or was it made of pine?"

"I don't really know, sir."

"What living relatives do you have? I'm thinking of Marion's security."

"I have a mother and two brothers, sir, but I haven't seen them for some time. As far as I know, they live in London, sir."

"Why don't you get on with your brothers?"

"Because they've bullied me all my life, sir."

"That's because you're a very weak man. You attract bullies. You are slow-witted and feeble," shouted the irascible undertaker.

"Another thing, will you kindly stop addressing me as 'sir'. It's unbelievably irritating. I'm a funeral director, not a schoolteacher.

"Do you expect my pupils to hurl India rubbers at me?"

The Reverend laughed nervously.

"Oh, please, Daddy!" interrupted Marion. "He's been ill. You really are intimidating him."

Her father showed the first sign of amusement during the conversation.

"He's just been out of hospital."

The Reverend was by now so nervous that he threw some salt over his shoulder.

"Will you please stop throwing bloody salt over your shoulder."

"I really am sorry, sir."

"The only people in hospitals I'm interested in are those I can send a man over to carrying a tape measure. Did you have anything wrong with you, which might occur, that is to say something nice and serious, like cancer, or a bad heart, that sort of brigade?"

"I'm really OK."

"Look here, my man. What the hell did I say about you refraining from calling me sir?"

"Oh, sorry."

"I can still get a little man to come out to measure you up."

"Psst! Daddy's only making a joke. That means you've got to laugh!"

"Ha! Ha! Ha!" said the Reverend, but the chuckle he gave was painful and forced.

"I'm talking seriously," said McManus after a pause, adding, "I'm afraid I'm getting on because I'm very ill and won't be around much longer. I need a replacement to ensure this firm's stability in its London offices."

He continued, "I think Marion is serious about you, although you are rather timid. You strike me as being a very serious person, despite your shyness."

McManus turned to the Reverend.

"Are you prepared to take a course in funeral direction?"

"It would be an honour, Mr McManus," said the Reverend, adding, "at least I'd like to try."

"Good, I'll have you enrolled into the Lear College of Funeral Direction and Embalmment in South London."

Eventually, the Reverend shook hands with McManus, who was much more friendly towards him suddenly.

The Reverend was allowed to go upstairs, where he slept in the spare room for a while. Marion joined him. It was she who woke him up.

***

As for McManus, the cancer which struck him down finally took hold and he died in his sleep.

Marion was heartbroken, despite her father's irascible spirit.

The nervous guest went to a nearby pub and drank alone. The crowd was particularly heavy, and he listened to other people's anecdotes to cheer himself up. A story, which he overheard while drinking, enthralled him particularly. It described a bus-driver, who was addicted to heroin.

The man had mad blue eyes and drove onto a roundabout. It was not long before he ended up in prison.

This was not the only incident which delighted the Reverend. William Stratisford, Harold's twin brother, married a foreign woman who didn't speak English. There was a banquet to celebrate the marriage.

At the end of the slowly served wedding meal, William's very mischievous son made a lot of raunchy remarks.

Natalie gazed across the vast table at a beautiful blond man and made advances towards him, but he spoke no English.

"What's he saying?" she asked her naughty nephew, William's son.

"Is there any chance of us going to a five-star hotel?" she asked the blond man.

"You are very beautiful," replied the man.

The beautiful blond man became besotted by Natalie's behaviour and asked her to go to bed with him.

William's stern father, Frederick, was furious with the blond man, and told his son in law that his services were no longer required in his family.

After a very long lunch, the Reverend rose to his feet and left the dining room. He was disgusted by the passes that Natalie was making at the blond man.

He had made a rapid decision and had decided that the person he really wanted to settle down with was none other than Natalie Klein.

My Darling Cockney Boy

The Reverend was amused by another of Natalie's anecdotes.

Following the death of her revered father, Kitty, her sex-crazed mother, married immediately. A deeply promiscuous woman, she galloped from dick to dick with the speed of an unfettered rottweiler.

One of her lovers was a prolific and dapper, tall cockney actor with thick fair hair, a straight nose and slightly tanned skin. Kitty had seen all his films on a regular basis when he had maintained his original accent.

She even went so far as to refer to him as "my darling cockney boy" in front of her family.

On one occasion, he turned up unannounced at the Klein's family house at seven o'clock in the evening, dressed immaculately in a navy-blue blazer, adorned with shining brass buttons as well as neatly creased, white trousers and polished co-respondent shoes.

Kitty's second husband answered the door. This was not the first time he had seen this man visiting the house.

"You" he said sternly, "I don't want to see you again. If you wish to see my wife, would you kindly take her to a hotel, rather than the matrimonial home."

"I apologise, sir, it won't happen again," replied the actor.

Natalie Klein and Dr Hennoch

Natalie told the Reverend a number of anecdotes when they went out together. She was bright and had been to university, where she gained a 2:2 in English.

There was an odious tutor who worked at the university. His name was Dr Hennoch and he was about 65 when he finally died. He taught students for *Prelims*, which took place within the first year. The tutorials were mixed.

Hennoch's personal appearance was repellent. He was red-faced, which suggested either that he had high blood pressure or that he had a drinking problem. He looked like a colossal eagle in profile, in that he had a huge, beaked nose, which was almost larger than he was.

No-one could understand what the hell he was talking about, although his "subject" appeared to be the alleged "motives" for an increase in capitalism in 17th-century Holland!

Some of the girls in his tutorials were timid, particularly when they were picked on by Dr Hennoch. They only guessed the answers required by him, having no idea what they were.

He failed to help them to find their words, in order to humiliate them. Many of them were reduced to floods of tears and left the room.

Eventually, it was Natalie's turn. She was determined not to be humiliated by this hideous, bird-like creature. He asked her yet another question, which was similar to the others.

His muddled question, related to what he called the economic deterioration of medieval France, as opposed to the economic remainder of seventeenth-century France.

Natalie was bored and unimpressed. She gave what she thought to be a reasonable answer, believing that Hennoch himself was having trouble understanding his "subject", so called.

He leant back arrogantly in his studded leather chair and crossed his legs at right angles.

"I'm afraid not!" he said.

Natalie was in a talkative mood.

"What are you afraid of?" she asked rudely.

There was a long pause.

"Miss Klein, following one of your more ghoulish essays which you handed in to me last week, I'd like to put another question to you."

"Yes? What is your question?"

"If you had lived at the time of the French Revolution, would you have been a *tricoteuse*?"

"No, I can't knit."

Dr Hennoch cleared his throat.

"I have another question to put to you, Miss Klein. If there were public hangings today, would you attend one?"

"That would depend entirely on whether or not I could find a parking space within fifty yards of the gallows," replied Natalie. She was beginning to wonder whether or not there was something wrong with her tutor's fucking gear.

She later found out that he was dying of cancer of the brain.